T^5
Tempted
Tried
Troubled
Transformed
Triumphed
In God's Time

JERLEAN S. NOBLE

ISBN-13: 978-0615619415

:

DEDICATION

To everything, there is a season, and a time to every purpose under the heaven. Ecclesiastes 3:1

Dedicated to my mother, Katie E. Cox, who went through the 5 T's with me. Yes, she did see the Triumph!

CONTENTS

Content's Continued

ACKNOWLEDGMENTS

To God be the Glory!

T^5 is a testimony of my journey from certain destruction to the safety of God's arms. It truly is in God's time when to reveal certain truths because He has placed someone here that needs it, that may be going through the same temptations, trials, and troubles, who need to be assured that it is a transformation and there is triumph in the end!

Thank you Nurse Pam, who as a student pursued me in the name of Jesus, to change my life and accept Jesus Christ as my personal Savior in a way that I never had. It was time to get serious and she had a mission with me.

TEMPTED

No temptation has overtaken you except what is common to mankind. God is faithful; he will not let you be tempted beyond what you can bear. But when you are tempted, He will also provide a way out so that you can endure it. 1 Corinthians 10:13

Temptation

Overwhelming temptation
was calling me
Dark voices, urges
Echoes from the deep

No fighting the feeling
No pulling away
Desires became stronger
Day after day

My will in question
My mind deplete
Wrong decisions driven
As deception took a seat

Lord, how do I escape
From sins gaping gate
Except through prayer
And a strong dose of faith

The Cookie Jar

Warning!
Stay away from the candy
Stay away from the cookie jar
Stay out of the street
Be in the house before dark
Like water that's deep
Like moths drawn to light
Something inside says
Search through the night
Get it
Jump
Go
I'm tempted.

Good Girl

I'll do what I'm told
I'll stay out of trouble
Because I'm strong
Responsible
Grown up
My own woman
I'm in control
But he's cute
He's older
He likes me
I want him
Caught up!

The Offer

Best friend
You've got it all
Good looks
Nice folks
Good home
Good-looking man
I'm your best friend
We share secrets
Trust me friend
Come into my world
One hit, one time
I got your back
Right!

Voices

Deceived
 I felt mindless
Like driftwood
On a beach
My unrest
A wet weight
That pooled around
My feet
The tide surged
The earth moved
Wobbly like the sea
My toes clutched
To damp surf
The fleeting grains beneath me

I was tempted
To stand still
To dare
The dark deep
Yet knowing
If I gave in
It would be to
Eternal sleep

Like the sweet pull
Of a bad boy
Like the lure of

Solomon's gold
I would flirt
And play hardball
Gambling with
My soul

Yet, I knew
The seduction
Beneath the
The rolling waves
The black voice
Whispering come
Was death's
Watery grave

Yet a small voice
 Bigger than the
Sea itself said
Live!

Praying

I'm praying, struggling
At the crossroads here
My will conflicted
My faith shy
I smile to the left
And nod to the right
Yet wrong seems strong
Wrong seems strong

Lord, just one more
Time I'm asking
Then I'll try to do what's right
Because You said
You'd forgive me
If I gave you the fight
I said
A-men

TRIED

That the trial of your faith, being much more precious than of gold that perisheth, though it be tried with fire, might be found unto praise and honour and glory at the appearing of Jesus Christ. 1st Peter 1:7

I Tried

Enough is enough
I can't take anymore
I'm tired of being slammed
I'm tired of closed doors

My family is gone
Lost all my real friends
I'm from pillar to post
For me there's no end

The image in the mirror
Is not who I am
I don't know that person
And I don't give a damn

Who's sorry for me
Who even cares
I may as well give in
To the urges that are there

I tried, I really tried

Sunday Morning

I went to church one Sunday
I promised my mom I would
Being saved didn't cross my mind
Since I never thought I could

The thing that shocked me most
While sitting in the pew
Was a child sitting close to me
Who said God has a plan for you

The Word came cutting through
And I was on my feet
My hands were in the air
As the Spirit spoke to me

I felt happy and elated
the tears fell like rain
As I yielded to the Savior
And my struggling life changed

Now I understand, I do
And I know what I know is true
That God has a laid out plan for all
As well as for me and you

Give in to the Savior today

Conviction

God said, your body's a temple
For my Holy Spirit to dwell
I can tell by your demeanor
That you're not doing well

You're not watching what you do
Or caring what you say
You're not listening for my call
Or trying to obey

You're easily persuaded
Without even giving thought
For what I sacrificed for you
Through the Blood on the Cross

So take this as a warning
This is notice of eviction
I'm kicking out your sins
And bringing about conviction

I thanked God for his patience
For holding tight to me
For breaking binding changes
For setting my soul free

Thank you Lord

God's Word

Let Your Word, Oh God, Your Word
Be my strength within the sun rays
Cushion the steps I make
Direct the road I take
Convict me of my mistakes

Be there when I close my eyes
Calm me when troubles rise
Speak out of how You save
Fill me with total praise

Be there to defend my faith
When storms make my world quake
Fill me when I kneel and pray
Guard me with Your mercy and grace

Let Your Word be a buffer for me
When my ship's on raging seas
Let me share with a sinner today
And to others You send my way

Be there when my day starts
Teach me to worship from my heart
To always be mindful of who you are
Fill my temple, and never part

Give me wisdom as I read each day
To rightly divide every Word You say

I'm Sick of Doing Wrong

In prayer I made promises
Lied to my family's face
Pretended change to real friends
Lived up to all the deadbeats
Who wanted to keep in the streets
I seem happy to end my dignity

This is me
 trying to regain
trying to maintain
To retain the person I was
The person I know God loves

Psalms 139: 1-4

Verse 1:
You have searched me, LORD, and you know me.
You have searched my heart
    You know the number of every beat
    Every thought of goodness
    And compassion for others

Verse 2 & 3
*You know when I sit and when I rise you perceive my
thoughts from afar. You discern my going out and my lying
down; you are familiar with all my ways.*
    You are here in the morning when I awake
    You're here if I slip into a nap
    You are there when I close my eyes for the night
    You are aware of my every move
    Though you are light years away
    from my furthest idea of where heaven is;
    You are here

Verse 4
*Before a word is on my tongue you, LORD, know it
completely.*
    When I think wrong of others
    And it's a passing or lingering thought
    When a curse word is there
    Or things of the flesh swell my heart
    When truth comes up and I want to deny
    Whatever I choose to do
    To you I cannot lie
    I cannot fathom the depth of your love
    I simply rest safe in the swells.

To be Like you Lord

I want to walk in places
 You've assigned me to go
Do things in a way
that is pleasing to you
I can only do it with your help.

    I love you Lord.

Heart to Heart

From the flood of my heart
The mouth speaks
The writer writes
Thoughts are shared
Feelings released
Remission takes place
The eyes reveal all
My heart thumps approval

I bear the truth of struggles
Of failings, defeat triumphs
God released me from hell
He is my redeemer
Truly the balm of Gilead
My testimony's another's victory
I'm saddened for those
who choose to die within
For I have been there too

To Win

No race is ever won
by stopping before the finish line
The treasure is always the next shovel down
Know that your alter is always before you
We conquer by continuing

TROUBLED

We are troubled on every side, yet not distressed; we are perplexed, but not in despair. 2nd Corinthians 4:8

In God's Time

Everything in God's time
Recoiled in my mind
God's Word, he preached
will keep you in line

Problems will rise
hold on for the ride
dark clouds will roll over
and the storm will subside

Things will work out granddaughter
In the Savior's time!"

God's Mercy

He makes the clouds his chariots
And rides on the wings of the wind . . .
He makes springs pour water into the ravines
It flows between the mountains
. . . And water all the beasts of the fields
Psalms 104: 3-4; 10-11

Who did I think I was to
Stand in the way of God's
Plans for me?

How dare I to presume
That my thoughtless plans would work
To destroy His temple with my carelessness
God, by sheer will
Could have put a stop
To my foolishness

And He did.

Mistake

Mistake's an excuse
For the risk I take
A justification
For decisions I make

One mistake
One incorrect turn
I find I'm destined
To crash and burn

Trouble's pending
Banging my door
Crawled up in a corner
Balled up on the floor

Worrying, crying
Overflowing tears
I put these scars here
That will not heal

God I need your blessings
Your mercy on me
It can't be as bad
As what it seem

Where are my morals
Why do I give in
Why do I find myself slipping
Again and again

I'm crying out now
Calling on my faith
I can't make it out
Without your grace
Help me Lord! Please!

Dust and Flowers

I stood there looking down
At the stone of my life
She bore me, loved me
In spite of my ways
I need her now
To accept my change
But there's only dust and flowers

I thought of God's Word
Just how we are formed
How to dust we'll return
'Cause from dust we were formed
How our days are like grass
When burned in the fields
Mom's life is over
She's not here to forgive--me
There's only dust and flowers
~The poem, a reminder of Psalms 103:16~

I Will Bless Your Name Lord

I am not a saint
But your Word is a keeper
And has ransomed me
from the fowlers snare
bless Your Word Lord God

When all was lost in my world
It was The Word that saved me
Your Word was always there
Always present

Like the ever present wind
Whether it roars like a mad storm
Or whispers like a soft breeze on
A Spring day, I knew you were there

I was selfish of you
Disrespectful of your presence
Though I still feared you
I felt Your gentleness

I knew you loved me Lord
More than I loved myself
You shielded me from
The destruction I tried to claim

That evilness that would
Seek to take my life
But You were there
Like the protective
Father of a naughty child
You saved me, yet again

The Word says you are
The Beginning and the End
The Alpha and the Omega
The Author and the Finisher of our faith

I see it every day
In every waking moment
In everything that moves
That lives and dies

I will bless You
I will praise You
It is because of these truths
That a I am comforted
In your love

What Now God?

I was thinking of questioning God one day
Got my thoughts together as to what I would say
Had a lot on my mind about this and that
But mostly, What now God?

I remembered how I made a mess of my life
How I cried to God as a battered wife
Then I thought how my husband just picked up and left
And I said, What now God?

I thought of my Big Ma, how sweet she had been
How in all I did she pushed me to win
And when she died how lost I felt
And I said, What now God?

Then my Daddy and also my Grandpa passed on
The rock of the family, the cornerstone
He and God had a special bond
I said Lord, What now God?

In the wrong direction my life took a swing
I started doing all kinds of crazy things
I found myself in a bottomless pit
I cried Lord, What now God?

Still spiraling, I drifted here and there
Saints I didn't know were sending up prayers
Then God said my child enough is enough
And drunk I said, What now God?

I lay in the dark in the stench of my sins
Then God breathed on me and the healing begin
I could feel the change as He opened my eyes
And again I said, What now God?

I allowed you to question my reason for things
Know all that you've gone through, there is a blood stain
My Son gave His life as a ransom for yours
That's what's now God

I bought you, I've saved you, I own your soul
Yet you question me, you are very bold
But my mercy is great and brand new every day
That's also what now God

When you were battered I saved your life
That's why you're no longer that man's wife
You have no scars but the ones in your mind
And I replaced them with memories of mine

And your Daddy, Big Ma and Grandpa gone on
Their time was up, so I brought them home
I was always there every time you cried
It was my compassion that dried your eyes

I love you and others you'll testify too
That's why I've allowed all that you've gone through
There's someone that's walking in your old shoes
Now you know my child just what you must do

There's a young girl whose falling just like you did
And a pusher who thinks that he's living big
I've placed you right where I need you to be
To testify and lead them both to me

I've dressed you for battle with the living Word

Go out and tell others and bring some to church
I replaced your fears with power from me
You're no longer enslaved, you've been set free

You were set aside to do all that you've done
All of your battles I've already won

Now I've answered you daughter
All the things that you've asked
I chose to mold you just for this task

There are souls that are hurting and waiting for you
I've equipped you my child
To do what you must do

There's no need to question
For all this was planned
I've always had you in the palm of my hand
Safe in my arms.

.

TRANSFORMED

Do not conform any longer to the pattern of this world, but be transformed by the renewing of your mind. Then you will be able to test and approve what God's will is--his good, pleasing and perfect will. Romans 12:2

Jesus Take the Wheel

Life's spiraling down
And I'm doing wrong
Disrespectful of friends
And bad turns me on

The Commandments of rule
The 10 laws of verse
Should guide me to do right
Yet I turn in reverse

It's not disrespect, Lord
I have for you
I'm just lost and confused
I don't know what to do

I've been punished and warned
I'm fighting the road
I'm stubborn, Combative,
Cunning and bold

Seems at every turn
My fates being sealed
Lord if this is a test
Please, Jesus take the wheel

The Testimony

In the peace of early dawn
God stirs me to my wake
I exalt the Lord on high
For His mercy and His grace

Overcome with compassion
Of His great love for me
Joy spill from my throat
Tears flow, I cannot see

My mind speaks against
The sin from whence I came
A prayer of confession
That cut and spew out pain

How it must have hurt the Savior
Time and time again
When I'd repent, then commit
The same old darkened sin

He could have left me dying
Let the devil have his way
With the things that I was doing
While throwing my life away

One day I chose to party
To ignore the warning signs
With alcohol and marijuana
I planned to have a good time

I was joking with the driver
Saying what we'd do that night
From the corner of my eye
A speeding car ran through the light

I remember ducking down
As the impact hit my door
Then my body started rising
As God pulled me from the floor

I hovered over the car
As I watched it spin around
Barely missing standing poles
And people on the ground

Make your choice I heard God say
Me or death what will you do
I felt the warmth of his great love
As I said Lord, I choose you

Then people started running
A shrilled siren filled the air
I looked sadly at my friend
Her face blank, as she just stared

Glass was in her head
Broken, I watched her bleed
I felt myself for injury
Not a scratch I had on me

It was then my set time came
God decided to change my track
Sent his angels to surround me
To minister and pull me back

Here's the way to the light
Or be left lying on your face
Your wrongs have been made right
I'm extending you my grace

So in humbleness and honor
I lay prostrate at his feet
Lifting arms and voice in praise
And God granted me His peace

Now I live and work for Him
Speaking, writing of his love
How He sent His Son to die
So we could be with Him above

Were it not for God's true vine
And the flow of Jesus Blood
I would not be the rose I am
I would have died a darkened bud
This is my testimony

Golden Manna

I expressed to God my hunger
I told him I could not see
The road I walked was dark and long
I was held by forces unseen
With his eyes His love consumed me
His compassion gave me strength
He commanded the waters to pour
The rain washed and made me clean
Then I received His blessings
The Word of life to succeed
For He said, "I am El-Shadi,"
And what I give you is all you need

And golden manna fell from heaven
Lighting the path for my feet to trod

Golden Manna (the story)

And golden manna fell from heaven lighting the path for my feet to trod."

The words were as clearly spoken to me as if there was someone was sitting across from me, talking to me, face to face. I lay half awake, 5:00 am, when those enlightened words came softly to my ear.

"Beautiful, that's beautiful Lord," I said.

I'd become accustomed to God's voice, giving me words, inspirational phrases to use in my poetry. I'd come to expect with the gift God gave me of writing, that often at early times in my morning devotion, there would be wonderful, filling, inspirational thoughts which would flood my heart with warmth, my mind with wisdom, and my eyes with tears of joy.

"Wow," I said, "I'd better write that down,"

… and I wondered how God would use me with it. Food from heaven, golden bread lighting the path for my feet to trod. I now know the manna was present in all of my trials and triumphs, and as I write this, I know why God spoke those words to me.

I've always known that only God can perform unique, supernatural miracles, as well as subtle feats. However, what I've never believed is, It could happen to me! Raised in a Christian home, there's no reason I shouldn't have stayed on the straight and narrow. Coming up I loved church and eagerly participated in activities and programs offered there. I learned long speeches, eloquently reciting them when called upon. At age 12, I received Christ as my Savior and was baptized by my proud Grandfather, Rev. John Henry Smith, who was the Pastor and founder of Mountain View Baptist Church, which I attended in Greenville, SC.

My great grandmother, Cora Raysor, of whom I called "Big Ma", raised me from a baby and died when I was 13. My mother took over but her agenda was different from the spiritual upbringing Big Ma afforded me. She could not handle me. The drastic change in my lifestyle took it's toll and I became rebellious and out of control. By 14, I was pregnant, 9 months later I gave birth to a baby boy.

My grandfather constantly warned me to pray and ask God to protect me or bad things would happen. However, there were unseen obstacles, and uncharted courses to plow. I was in a centrifugal spin, pulled into the hole of ever deepening sin. I was totally sucked in. Nevertheless, God had a plan for me; He put me on a course that would change my life forever.

At age 21 I married a drug addict. God warned me but my eyes were closed, my ears shut. It was the early 70's and heroin was relatively new to SC. My husband was hooked, and I followed suit. He was abusive, both physically and mentally. I thought by staying with him I'd please him and he would change. I supported both our habits by becoming a thief. We moved from SC to Boston, I decided to go to business school, hoping to stop this slide to death. My fate was not in my hands. I overdosed several times, while untrained addicts shot salt in my veins to revive me. God was there all the time. He had a mission for me and I was going to live, regardless of my destructive lifestyle.

Nine years of fear and abuse took its toll on me and we finally separated. I tried to pick up the pieces, to start anew but I still had a ways to go. In 1978 I met someone else--someone who turned out to be worse than the husband I had. He too was into drugs and I plunged back, head first. Falling, this time to the bottom of the barrel. I ended in a run for my life. I fled but was turned in by my new boyfriend to save himself. Upon being incarcerated, I felt strangely at ease. Somehow, I knew God was about to deal with me, I didn't blame him for my mess, I thanked Him. I knew he had saved my life that I would've been dead had he left me in the world.

Out of two years time, I did eight months; time enough for my spirit to settle down, for me to be still and know of God. I joined the choir, started reading the Bible, and learned to cry out to God. He blessed and delivered me. Upon release God began to open doors. Things eased and I became comfortable in my zone, too comfortable. I backslid. God had delivered me from the clutches of heroin but I became prey to other drugs. Still, my God held on, still lighting the path for my feet to trod.

Thinking of all of my lost loves, I began to drink and smoke my problems away. Little did I know God was about to end my slide of destruction, but I was still hell bent on having my way-- the snake was coiled to strike. I thought I'd found strength in the bottle. With 2 straight shots of vodka and a the added high of a strong joint, I got into my car to look for a another woman's man who had left me.

Muddled and feeling wronged, I totaled my car. For my stupidity, I was rewarded with a head concussion and the lost my front teeth. The enemy was out to kill me, but God was in control. Yet still, I was as hardheaded and stiff-necked as the children of Israel in Moses time. At the hospital I was checked for other injuries. Miraculously, neither alcohol nor drugs were detected. I was released from the hospital, and was never charged in the accident.

The Voice

Ten days later, I was at work, excited for the Christmas holidays. A friend came by and wanted to get high, my adrenalin began to run. The urge was so great I became wild; 5:00 was too far away; my paycheck was burning my pocket and I had to leave. The fib I told my supervisor was so great I started to believe it myself. Victorious, I gathered my things, got into the car with my friend, picked up the drugs and it was on!

...choose ye this day, whom you will serve...Joshua 24:15

The Decision

The drive home was antsy. My purse was loaded with all we needed to reach that all-important high. I had cocaine (about $300 worth), an ounce of marijuana, 2 bottles of wine and cognac to wash it all down when I got home. Approaching the intersection, the light changed from red to green for us. I glanced to the right at a speeding car heading straight at me. Oh my God!! WHAM! The car hit the door at which I sat. I went down. The next thing I remember is being high above the car—looking down at the accident, seeing the whole wreck as it happened. I witnessed it spinning out of control. I heard a voice say to me "Is it me or death? Make your choice." I said, God it's you. It's you. As I'm writing this, the tears are brimming my eyes. I was not hurt, I felt a little pain in my back but soon knew there was not a scratch, not a bruise on me. How could this be as the entire wreck happened on my side? Although the wreck was not our fault, we did not receive a dime because God had this accident happen to a turn my life around and I accepted it. I did not go to the hospital. There were two inquisitive elderly ladies at the scene of the accident who gave me a ride to my apartment.

Therefore, if any man be in Christ, he is a new creature, old things have passed away, all things have become new. 2 Corinthians 5:17

The Manna Revealed

Even as I hovered between hell and salvation, the hell hounds were pulling at my soul. I tried to recapture the flesh, that high that enslaved me for the better part of 4 years. I said Lord, one more time and I won't do this again. I did, but could not get high, I could not enjoy it.

God had breathed into me a new man, a Spirit man that began to change my life. God begin to speak to the demon that sought to imprison me forever, and God said NOT SO! I knew my journey was over. I was happy. I gathered all the paraphernalia and threw it out; I cleaned out my house. I got on my knees and asked God to forgive me and to save me and he did. He washed my slate clean, gave me the thirst for the Word, took away the cravings for drugs, alcohol and the cigarettes.

I am now in a progressive ministry, I am a self-professed poet and writer. I write this a clean, drug free woman. It has now been 25 years, praise the Lord. All along the golden manna fed me, washed me, watched over me and was a cushion for me every time I fell. …

And golden manna fell from heaven lighting the path for my feet to trod. Thank God.

The Red Thread

In a vision the Lord made me a dress
Woven of fine red cloth
Sewn together piece by piece
From neckline, to bodice, to hem
Each piece carefully put together
According to His love
It was beautiful

I was but a child in the vision
And as I grew so did the dress
Never losing shape, never fraying
It was full of the Spirit of God
In the dress I was warm and comfortable

As I entered adolescent years
The illusion of the world was upon me
I loved the flesh and its offerings
And so the dress fell away
Piece by piece by piece

I was chilled, my body cold
I was alone, I needed a friend
I prayed forgive me, I'm sorry
And then I'd slip again

The years of sin took over
And in my stupor of shame
I felt a tugging at my soul
I looked down and saw a string

A red string that clung to me
So I traced it for it felt warm
I could feel a radiant Holy power
Coming from the hand of God

I was glad he had not left me
But, I was hanging on by a thread
I remembered, God once told me
The wages of sin is death

God said I'll never leave you
Because of the mess you're in
Remember up on Calvary
My Son died for your sins

I understood the sacrifice
Of the thorns that crowned his head
Of the blood that trickled down his face
It was the thread--that was the thread

I thanked Him for His mercy
I realized, I am blessed
Then afar I heard some sewing
God was making me a new dress

Stitch, stitch, stitch
The neckline,
The sleeves all came in place
Glory to your name Lord
I thank you for your grace

I knew as the blood covered my soul
I belonged to God forevermore

The stitching got louder and faster
I saw the spear plunge in His side,
the waist, then the skirt came into view,
All I could do was cry

Hope was born, my faith renewed
I rejoiced as the dress returned
But, when the hem began to appear
The stitching slowed down again

Will you surrender your heart?
Your mind?
Will you surrender your will?
Will you let me fight your battles
Rule your life, your peace to be still
Stitch, stitch, stitch
Stop crying you're not to blame
Stitch, stitch, stitch
Your life will never be the same

God said,
'Old sins have passed away
All things have become new'
Thank God for the Blood.

TRIUMPHED

Therefore, if any man is in Christ, he is a new creature: old things have passed away; behold, all things have become new. 2 Corinthians 5:17

I Understand Now Lord

When disobeying meant pleasing my friends
More than hurting my mom
When sneaking off to do wrong
Meant more than staying in
And doing my chores

When falling in a hole so deep
With walls too slick and disgusting to hold on to
When there was no ground to stand on
When everything around me was dark

And the only breath
I heard was my own
All my hope was gone
All my emotions spent

No mama to run to
No daddy
No friends or relatives
No one meant me any good--no one was there

When I was cocooned in a self made hell
Eyes woven shut
Mouth stunk with disrespect
and there no warmness or love inside

When I couldn't struggle to feel any of it
And I was at the bottom with no way out
There was only one beam of light
One ray that cut through

One ray that begin to cut away
And soften the bind around my hands
My ears popped just long enough
To hear You Lord whisper my name

A warm tear lined the bottom
of my eyes, rolled down my face
Moistened my mouth
So I could whisper
Lord! Help me please.
I'm sorry
I want to be whole again,
I want to be free to speak
Spread joy and love about you
Have a vision to do right
to be respectful
I understand God. I do.

The sincerity of my prayer,
The wetness from the tears
The warmth from God's love
Cut through my dismay
His Joy., His Peace, breathed life in me
I understand now God
I do

Inseparable Blood

Bless the cross of Calvary
And It's Blood forever shelter us
And may His eternal Holiness
Cover the Body of Christ

For when the saving blood was shed
The only color seen was red
So powerful it covered all
The multitudes of sin
And every race, creed and color
This world has within

The same Blood still prevails
Though there are those who seek to assail
And come between and separate
The race God made as one
One race, inseparable, under the Blood
One God, One Blood, One Baptism

Brand New

When I was in sin
You did not forsake me
While I was stubborn
You didn't give up
In my doubt
You renewed my faith
When bound you set me free
When I fell
You picked me up
My tears you wiped away
When I cried out
you heard and blessed me
when I was lost
you showed me the way

Now I believe what I couldn't believe
I understand what I could not conceive
I see now what I couldn't see
I pray to be one with you God

I now step where I could not go
Speak out what I couldn't say
I pray what I could not pray
All because of you God

I'm praising instead of cursing
Singing glorious songs to you
Dancing and worshiping in the spirit
All because of you God

It was Jesus blood that saved me
The Blood that made me whole
By your mercy I've been forgiven Lord
My dark heart now shines as gold

I claim you Sweet Jesus
I exalt and acknowledge you
If not for your grace and mercy
There's no way I could have come through

'If any man be in Christ he is a new creature'
I am brand new

Dawning Peace

So awesome is thy presence Oh God
So Holy thy universal reign
Thou speak through the folds of darkest night
Commanding the dawn to open
The sun to slowly rise
Shedding the cloak of twilight
Revealing panoramic brushes of gold, bronze and purple
Ascending the expanse of firmament
A coronation of transcendent beauty
Trailing your train of glory
The angels flutter not their wings
All is quiet in your wake

The view of David is made plain
In wonder of your majesty at Mizpah
My eyes water at the Carolina sky
Breathtaking in its splendor
There is something about the peace
Of the morning
When God opens up the day

Morning Glory

A point of light pierce the darkness
Fanning out into a holy brilliance
Of kaleidoscopic colors
An awe-inspiring phenomenon
Transforming the firmament
Into a panorama of inexplicable,
Eye watering, beauty
A raw power, unseen, by man,
By his thoughts and even
The poets pen
At that moment, that precise second
All is still and quiet
In the air, the desert,
The mountains, upon the face of waters
God's creatures bow down
In homage to Shekinah Glory
It is His time of passing
It is a time of worship
Praise Ye the Lord!

Private Time (a prayer)

Lord in my private time
In my solemn time of prayer
As I enter in your presence
Let me to humble, crumble there

I shut out the world behind
For Your Blood dear Lord I plead
I find comfort at your Holy feet
Where You've made room for me

It is here that I'm restored
By your Spirit I'm endowed
Here I lay, confess my sins to you
The things I have allowed

I beseech You Holy Spirit
I lay prostrate before thee
As your countenance fill this room
Please Lord hover over me

It's amazing what I'm feeling here
The sweetness of your breath
Assuring me I'm safe from harm
From injury and from death

I thank You for amazing grace
For all you do for me
For your blessed Shekinah Glory
Lord I stretch my hand to thee

Oh Great Jehovah Jireh
How can I make things right
Give me a fresh anointing
Make me precious in your sight

Now minister to me Jesus
Guide me through the storms and rain
Accept this humble prayer now
Heal and take away the pain

All glory and honor to you
As I end this prayer and praise
May your Blood forever keep your saints
Forever and always

My Word, My Friend

In the beginning was the Word
And the Word was with God
And the Word was God
The same was in the beginning with God
John 1:1-2

I have a Holy Bible,
It's name now faintly seen
It's body worn, torn,
Pulled from the covers
That bind it to me.

It is taped and soiled with tears,
With secrets, confessions, and promises

Most of all love
It is my closest friend?

We come together at dawns stillness,
It's enclosed in my secret place
The power of God so strong, so real
I'm full as I near the door

At times without words, all is said
At contact, I clutch, hold close
The force so genuine to me
As I speak from my iniquities

Often my storms overwhelm me
The rains flood the seas of my eyes
They spill from my soul's reservoir
Be it joy, sorrow, or strife

The Word of God is filling
Pure bread of heaven's food
I kiss the pages when I'm through,
My lips stick, wet from weeping

I close my eyes and linger there
The pages kiss me back
I have felt His arms around me
An assured "I got you" love

I have a Bible I carry to church
To bible studies and such
But not this one

I do not want it fixed.
It is my true companion,
My special friend.

It holds the Living Word
It holds my very life.
I carry it on long trips
To places where I spend the night

It is what I reach for in budding dawn
To spill my soul upon
To pour out my woes, my joys
In tears and laughter

It is sacred, this commune with God
With the Trinity

Through worn, torn, tear-stained pages
My beat-up friend
Opened the highway to God
Introduced me to Jesus, who accepts me
Just as I am

When life has passed me by
And my journey is at end
Place within my still hands
My friend

Woman of God

Charm is deceptive, and beauty is fleeting; but a woman who
fears the Lord is to be praised.
Proverbs 31:30 (NIV)

What does it take to be a woman of God,
To walk proudly in His favor?
To stand that others may see his grace--
In your joy and in your labor

What does it take to be a woman of God,
To hold high your head with pride
Knowing that His Word is forever true,
In His arms you're safe to abide

He says in His Word, 'Know that I am God,'
I am here, I hear your pleas
Just seek my face & humble yourself;
In you I will plant my seed

I AM the true vine, my Father the gardener'
You're the fruit that I bear, you see.
Abide in me,
And keep my Word '
'I'll supply your every need.'

It is good to be a
Woman of God

The seed is the Word of God
Luke 8:11

He Is

He is my morning Java
He is my cup of tea
He is the ray of sunshine
That stroke me through the trees

He is the soft and mellow sound
So gentle and so sweet
Before sun up He sings to me
A Holy melody

He is my bright and morning star
He is my guiding light
He is the strong and mighty power
That protect me through the night

He is my Rose of Sharon
He is my El-Shadi
He is Jehovah Jireh
Who for my sins did die

He is Jehovah Rapha
The merciful God that heals
He is Jehovah Shalom
His glorious peace I feel

He guards the gateways to my heart
I feel His Spirit there
I love to call Him by His name
When I kneel down in prayer

I call Him God the Father
The Son and Holy Ghost
I call Him Precious Savior
He's the Shepherd at the door

He is the Ram in the bush
He's the Holy Sacrifice
Without the shedding of His blood
There's no way, truth, nor life

He's all and everything to me
With Him my life's a plus
I stand a witness for his Love
I call Him The Lamb,

A Little Bird's Morning Prayer

This morning outside my window
Before the break of dawn
As I kneeled before The Lord in prayer
I heard a lovely song

God beckoned me to listen
As the notes were tailored fine
The flawless sound was lovely
There was no need to rhyme

The repetitiveness then intensified
I could feel it deep inside
The sound was so angelic
I closed my eyes and cried

The sound was from a small bird
Perched at my window pane
It was his time of worship
So he lifted his voice to sang

I thank You for Your goodness God
I thank You for Your grace
I thank for Your favor
You've granted me for this day

I thank for the breakfast You
So thoughtfully left for me
I thank You for this branch I'm on
For the nest here in this tree

I thank You for this voice
Though small it may be
It just enough and all I need
To praise and glorify Thee

I listened quite intensely
As his little voice filled the air
I ended my prayer and thanked the Lord
For letting me be there

To hear the little humble bird
As he sang his morning prayer
God said
'Let everything that has breath Praise ye the Lord!'

What's In a Name?

HE IS
GOD
Alpha and Omega -
The Beginning and the End
I Am that I AM, God the Father, God the Son,
God the Holy Spirit, The Lord Thy God

EXALT HIM
PRAISE HIM
LOVE HIM
Jehovah, El Shaddai, Sovereign Lord, Christ The Lord,
Merciful Savior

ACKNOWLEDGE HIM
Father
Ancient Of Days
Holy One, Son Of God,
Son Of Man, The Lamb, Rose Of Sharon, Lilly Of The
Valley,
Everlasting Father, Prince Of Peace, The Word, Glorious
God, Son Of David, King Of Kings,
Bright And Morning Star, Mighty God, Christ, Risen Savior,
Emanuel, Wonderful, Counselor, The God Of Abraham,
Isaac, And Jacob, The Lord God Of Your Fathers, The Rock,
The Fortress, The Deliverer, True Vine,
The Gardener, The Light
My Salvation.

GLORIFY HIM
DEPEND ON HIM
MAGNIFY HIM

El Elyon,, The Most High God,
El Shaddai, The All-Sufficient One
Adonai, Lord, Master
El Olam, The Everlasting God
Elohim, Creator
Yahweh, Lord (Jehovah)
Qanna, The Everlasting God
Jehovah - Jireh, The Lord Will Provide
Jehovah - Nissi, The Lord, My Banner
Jehovah - Raah, The Lord, My Shepherd
Jehovah - Rapha, The Lord That Healeth
Jehovah - Sabaoth, The Lord Of Hosts,
Jehovah - Shalom, The Lord Is Peace
Jehovah - Shammah, The Lord Is There
Jehovah - Mekoddishkem
The Lord Who Sanctifies You
Jehovah - Tsidkenu
The Lord, Our Righteousness
The Shepherd, The Bread Of Life

CALL HIM
JESUS

ABOUT THE AUTHOR

Jerlean Smith Noble is now retired from the University of South Carolina in Columbia, SC. She is a wife, mother, and grandmother. Though born in Greenville, SC, she's made Columbia her home. She enjoys church, family and work. She and her organization has made outreach it's mission sponsoring programs for homeless children, incarcerated women, and at-risk youth. She feels responsible to those whom she feels God has led her to help. She enjoys success as an author and poet. At present she has been published in local magazines and is working on her ancestral history through research in Ancestry.com.

To her credit she's written and published 5 books:
Big Mama and Me, Simple Recipes, The History & Commemoration of the Palmetto State Law Enforcement Officers Association, Tin Can: The Slitting Edge (New) and now, T5 – In God's Time, her first published book of inspirational poetry.

She has Co-authored: Wordz Up: A Story To Tell, and Potpourri,

She has two new books in progress:
Beulah Blue and In God's Time.
Owy Owl & The Magic Apple Vine
Owy Owl Learns to Count

She was selected as a contributing author in The Writer's Net: Anthology of Prose, Vol. I, edited by Gary D. Kessler. Jerlean is also President and founder of the Columbia Writer's Alliance, a 501(c)3 organization now in it's eighth year (www.colawriters.com).